CONTENTS

BEST-LOVED RHYMES

FAVOURITE FOLK

ANIMAL FRIENDS

PLAYING TOGETHER

This book belongs to

....

CLASSIC TREASURY

NURSERY RHYMES

Miles Kelly

First published in 2014 by Miles Kelly Publishing Ltd
Harding's Barn, Bardfield End Green, Thaxted, Essex, CM6 3PX, UK

2 4 6 8 10 9 7 5 3 1

Publishing Director Belinda Gallagher
Creative Director Jo Cowan
Editorial Director Rosie Neave
Editor Fran Bromage
Designers Jo Cowan, Joe Jones
Production Manager Elizabeth Collins
Reprographics Stephan Davis, Jennifer Cozens, Thom Allaway

ISBN 978-1-78209-581-1

Printed in China

British Library Cataloguing-in-Publication Data
A catalogue record for this book is available from the British Library

ACKNOWLEDGEMENTS
The publishers would like to thank the following artists
who have contributed to this book:
Cover
Central image: Sharon Harmer at The Bright Agency
Other elements: Alice Brisland at The Bright Agency, LenLis/Shutterstock.com,
kusuriuri/Shutterstock.com, Lana L/Shutterstock.com, Markovka/Shutterstock.com

Inside pages
Advocate Art: Angela Muss, Hannah Wood, Helen Poole, Luciana Feito, Marco Furlotti
The Bright Agency: Lindsey Sagar
Frank Endersby
All other artwork from the Miles Kelly Artwork Bank

Made with paper from a sustainable forest

www.mileskelly.net
info@mileskelly.net

TASTY TREATS

OUT AND ABOUT

NUMBER RHYMES

WHATEVER THE WEATHER

BEDTIME RHYMES

STORY TIME

we'll all have some tea

BEST-LOVED RHYMES

Have you any wool?

Oh, the grand old Duke of York

Old Macdonald had a Farm

Old Macdonald had a farm,
E-I-E-I-O!
And on that farm he had
some cows, E-I-E-I-O!
With a moo-moo here,
And a moo-moo there,
Here a moo, there a moo,
Everywhere a moo-moo,
Old Macdonald had a farm,
E-I-E-I-O!

Old Macdonald had a farm, E-I-E-I-O!
And on that farm he had some sheep, E-I-E-I-O!
With a baa-baa here,
And a baa-baa there,
Here a baa, there a baa,
Everywhere a baa-baa,
Old Macdonald had a farm, E-I-E-I-O!

Old Macdonald had a farm, E-I-E-I-O!
And on that farm he had some ducks, E-I-E-I-O!
With a quack-quack here,
And a quack-quack there,
Here a quack, there a quack,
Everywhere a quack-quack,
Old Macdonald had a farm,
E-I-E-I-O!

Old Macdonald had a farm, E-I-E-I-O!
And on that farm he had some pigs, E-I-E-I-O!
With an oink-oink here,
And an oink-oink there,
Here an oink, there an oink,
Everywhere an oink-oink,
Old Macdonald had a farm, E-I-E-I-O!

Humpty Dumpty

Humpty Dumpty sat on a wall,
Humpty Dumpty had a great fall;
All the king's horses
and all the king's men
Couldn't put Humpty
together again.

See-saw, Margery Daw

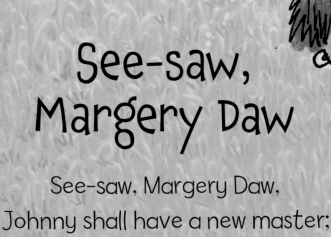

See-saw, Margery Daw,
Johnny shall have a new master;
He shall have but a penny a day,
Because he can't work any faster.

Little Miss Muffet

Little Miss Muffet
Sat on a tuffet,
Eating her curds and whey;
Along came a spider,
Who sat down beside her,
And frightened Miss Muffet away.

Pat-a-Cake

Pat-a-cake, pat-a-cake, baker's man,
Bake me a cake as fast as you can.
Pat it and prick it, and mark it with 'B',
And put it in the oven
For Baby and me.

Baa, Baa, Black Sheep

Baa, baa, black sheep,
Have you any wool?
Yes, sir, yes, sir,
Three bags full:
One for the master,
And one for the dame,
And one for the little boy
Who lives down the lane.

Mary's Lamb

Mary had a little lamb,
Its fleece was white as snow;
And everywhere that Mary went
The lamb was sure to go.

It followed her to school one day,
That was against the rules.
It made the children laugh and play,
To see a lamb at school.

Jack and Jill

Jack and Jill went up the hill
To fetch a pail of water;
Jack fell down and broke his crown,
And Jill came tumbling after.

Up Jack got, and home did trot,
As fast as he could caper.
He went to bed,
To mend his head
With vinegar and brown paper.

Hickory, Dickory, Dock

Hickory, dickory, dock!
The mouse ran up the clock.
The clock struck one,
The mouse ran down,
Hickory, dickory, dock!

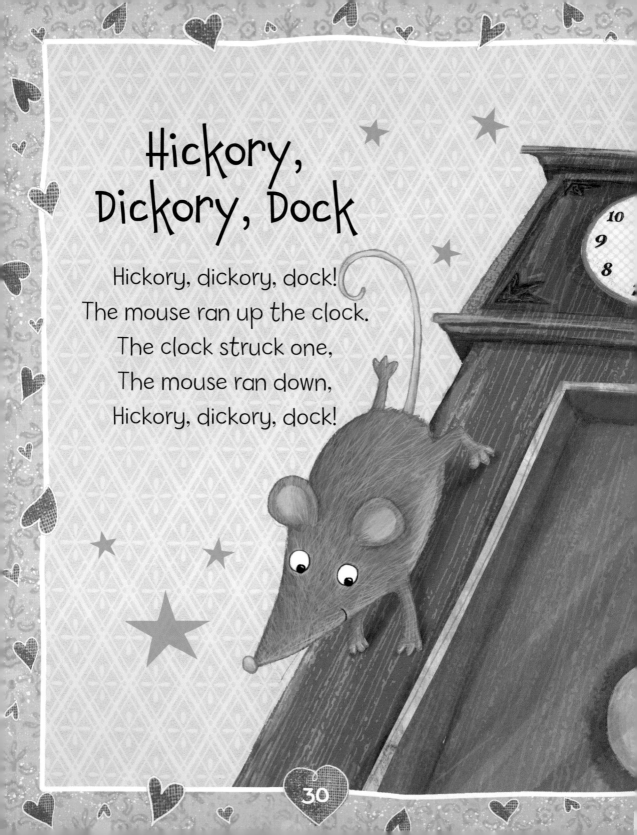

Hickory, dickory, dock!
The mouse ran up the clock.
The clock struck two,
The mouse said, "Boo!"
Hickory, dickory, dock.

Hickory, dickory, dock!
The mouse ran up the clock.
The clock struck three,
The mouse said, "Weeee!"
Hickory, dickory, dock.

Hickory, dickory, dock!
The mouse ran up the clock.
The clock struck four,
Let's sing some more!
Hickory, dickory, dock.

Hey Diddle Diddle

Hey diddle diddle,
The cat and the fiddle,
The cow jumped over the moon;
The little dog laughed
To see such fun,
And the dish ran away with the spoon.

Duke of York

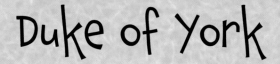

Oh, the grand old Duke of York,
He had ten thousand men;
He marched them up to the top of the hill,
And he marched them down again.

And when they were up, they were up,
And when they were down, they were down.
And when they were only halfway up,
They were neither up nor down.

Little Bo-Peep

Little Bo-Peep has lost her sheep,
And doesn't know where to find them;

Leave them alone
and they'll come home,
Bringing their tails
behind them.

Monday's Child

Monday's child is
fair of face,

Tuesday's child is
full of grace,

Wednesday's child is
full of woe,

Thursday's child has
far to go,

Friday's child is
loving and giving,

Saturday's child works
hard for a living,

But the child that is born
on the Sabbath day,
Is bonny and blithe
and good and gay.

Mary, Mary

Mary, Mary, quite contrary,
How does your garden grow?
With silver bells and cockle shells,
And pretty maids all in a row.

Polly, put the kettle on

Polly, put the kettle on,
Polly, put the kettle on,
Polly, put the kettle on,
We'll all have tea.

Sukey, take it off again,
Sukey, take it off again,
Sukey, take it off again,
They've all gone away.

Bye baby bunting, Father's gone a-hunting

FAVOURITE FOLK

Here I am,
Little jumping Joan

There was an Old Man with a beard

Little Boy Blue

Little Boy Blue,
Come blow your horn,
The sheep's in the meadow,
The cow's in the corn.

But where is the boy
Who looks after the sheep?
He's under a haystack,
Fast asleep!

Will you wake him?
No, not I,
For if I do,
He'll surely cry.

Lucy Locket

Lucy Locket lost her pocket,
Kitty Fisher found it;
Not a penny was there in it,
But a ribbon round it.

There was a Crooked Man

There was a crooked man,
And he walked a crooked mile,
He found a crooked sixpence
Upon a crooked stile;
He bought a crooked cat,
Which caught a crooked mouse,
And they all lived together
In a little crooked house.

The Old Woman who Lived in a Shoe

There was an old woman
who lived in a shoe,
She had so many children
she didn't know what to do.
She gave them some broth
without any bread,

Then told them all
off and sent them
to bed.

Curly Locks

Curly Locks, Curly Locks,
Wilt thou be mine?
Thou shalt not wash dishes,
Nor yet feed the swine;

But sit on a cushion,
And sew a fine seam,
And feed upon strawberries,
Sugar and cream.

Bye Baby Bunting

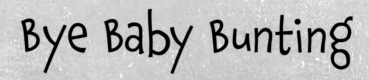

Bye baby bunting,
Father's gone a-hunting,
To get a little rabbit skin,
To wrap his little baby in.

Little Girl, Little Girl

Little girl, little girl,
Where have you been?
Gathering roses
To give to the queen.

Little girl, little girl,
What gave she you?
She gave me a diamond
As big as my shoe.

There was an Old Man

There was an Old Man with a beard,
Who said, "It is just as I feared!
Two Owls and a Hen,
Four Larks and a Wren,
Have all built their nests
in my beard."

Edward Lear
1812–88, b. England

O Dear, what can the Matter be?

O dear, what can the matter be?
Dear, dear, what can the matter be?
O dear, what can the matter be?
Johnny's so long at the fair.

He promised to bring me a basket of posies,
A garland of lilies, a garland of roses,
A little straw hat, to set off the ribbons
That tie up my bonny brown hair.

Jumping Joan

Here I am,
Little jumping Joan;
When nobody's with me
I'm all alone.

Here is the Church

Here is the church,
And here is the steeple,
Open the door and see all the people.
Here is the parson going upstairs,
And here he is saying his prayers.

Father's Day

"Walk a little slower, Daddy,"
said a child so small.
"I'm following in your footsteps
and I don't want to fall.

Sometimes your steps are very fast,
Sometimes they're hard to see;
So, walk a little slower, Daddy,
For you are leading me.

Someday when I'm all grown up,
You're what I want to be;
Then I will have a little child
Who'll want to follow me.

And I would want to lead just right,
And know that I was true;
So walk a little slower, Daddy,
For I must follow you."

Author unknown

Jack be Nimble

Jack be nimble,
Jack be quick,
Jack jump over the candlestick.

Lavender's Blue

Lavender's blue, dilly, dilly,
Lavender's green,
When I am King, dilly, dilly,
You shall be Queen.

Who told you so, dilly, dilly,
Who told you so?
'Twas my own heart, dilly, dilly,
That told me so.

Call up your men, dilly, dilly,
Set them to work,
Some to the plough, dilly, dilly,
Some to the cart.

Some to make hay, dilly, dilly,
Some to make corn,
While you and I, dilly, dilly
Keep ourselves warm.

Lavender's green, dilly, dilly,
Lavender's blue,
If you love me, dilly, dilly,
I will love you.

Little Polly Flinders

Little Polly Flinders
Sat among the cinders,
Warming her pretty little toes.

Her mother came and caught her,
And told off her little daughter
For spoiling her nice new clothes.

Old King Cole

Old King Cole was a merry old soul,
And a merry old soul was he;
He called for his pipe,
And he called for his bowl,
And he called for his fiddlers three.

Every fiddler had a fine fiddle,
And a very fine fiddle had he.
Oh, there's none so rare,
As can compare
With King Cole and his fiddlers three!

There was a Little Girl

There was a little girl, and she had a little curl,
Right in the middle of her forehead;
When she was good, she was very, very good,
But when she was bad, she was horrid!

Dance to your Daddy

Dance to your daddy,
My bonnie laddy,
Dance to your daddy,
My bonnie lamb.

You shall have a fishy,
In a little dishy,
You shall have a fishy,
When the boat comes in.

Dance to your daddy,
My bonnie laddy,
Dance to your daddy,
And to your mammy sing.

You shall get a coatie,
And a pair of breekies,
You shall get a coatie,
When the boat comes in.

There was an Old Woman

There was an old woman
Tossed up in a basket,
Seventeen times as high as the moon.
Where she was going
I just had to ask it,
For in her hand she carried a broom.

"Old woman, old woman, old woman," said I,
"O whither, O whither, O whither so high?"
"I'm sweeping the cobwebs
Down from the sky!
And I'll be with you
By and by."

I've been to London,
To visit the queen

ANIMAL FRIENDS

She wanders lowing here and there

So whene'er you meet a crocodile

What does the Bee do?

What does the bee do?
Bring home honey.
And what does Father do?
Bring home money.
And what does Mother do?
Lay out the money.
And what does baby do?
Eat up the honey.

Christina Rossetti
1830–94, b. England

87

Goosey, Goosey Gander

Goosey, goosey gander,
Whither shall I wander?
Upstairs and downstairs
And in my lady's chamber.

There I met an old man
Who would not say his prayers;
So I took him by his left leg
And threw him down the stairs.

Cock-a-Doodle-Doo

Cock-a-doodle-doo!
My dame has lost her shoe,
My master's lost his fiddling stick,
And doesn't know what to do.

Cock-a-doodle-doo!
My dame has found her shoe,
My master's found his fiddling stick,
So cock-a-doodle-do!

Little Robin Redbreast

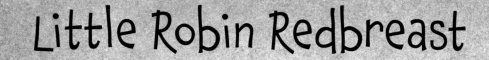

Little Robin Redbreast sat upon a tree,
Up went pussy cat, and down went he!
Down came pussy cat, and away Robin ran;
Says little Robin Redbreast, "Catch me if you can!"

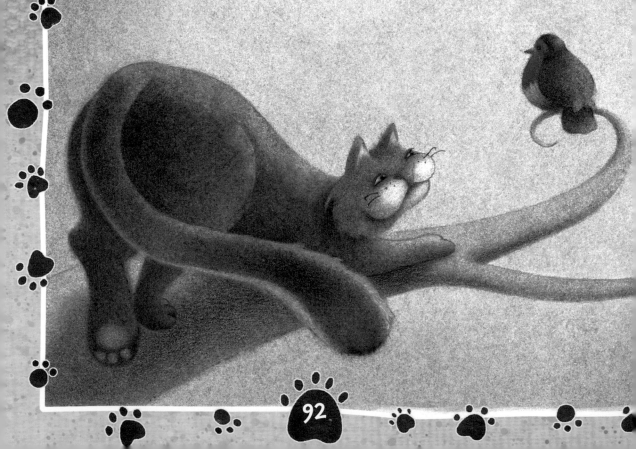

Little Robin Redbreast jumped upon a spade,
Pussy cat jumped after him,
and then he was afraid.
Little Robin chirped and sang,
and what did Pussy say?
Pussy cat said, "Mew, mew, mew,"
and Robin jumped away.

Little Robin Redbreast jumped upon a wall,
Pussy cat jumped after him,
and almost got a fall!
Little Robin chirped and sang,
and what did Pussy say?
Pussy cat said, "Mew," and Robin flew away.

A Cat came Fiddling

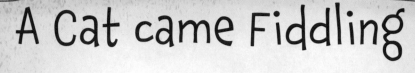

A cat came fiddling out of a barn,
With a pair of bagpipes under her arm.
She could sing nothing but fiddle dee dee,
The mouse has married the bumblebee.
Pipe, cat; dance, mouse;
We'll have a wedding at our good house.

Ducks' Ditty

All along the backwater,
Through the rushes tall,
Ducks are a-dabbling.
Up tails all!

Ducks' tails, drakes' tails,
Yellow feet a-quiver,
Yellow bills all out of sight
Busy in the river!

Slushy green undergrowth
Where the roach swim
Here we keep our larder,
Cool and full and dim.

Everyone for what he likes!
We like to be
Heads down, tails up,
Dabbling free!

High in the blue above
Swifts whirl and call
We are down a-dabbling
Up tails all!

Kenneth Grahame
1859–1932, b. Scotland

97

The Cow

The friendly cow all red and white,
I love with all my heart.
She gives me cream with all her might,
To eat with apple tart.
She wanders lowing here and there,
And yet she cannot stray,
All in the pleasant open air,
The pleasant light of day;
And blown by all the winds that pass
And wet with all the showers,
She walks among the meadow grass
And eats the meadow flowers.

Robert Louis Stevenson
1850–94, b. Scotland

Pussy Cat Mole

Pussy Cat Mole
Jumped over a coal
And in her best petticoat
Burnt a great hole.

Poor pussy's weeping,
She'll have no more milk
Until her best petticoat's
Mended with silk.

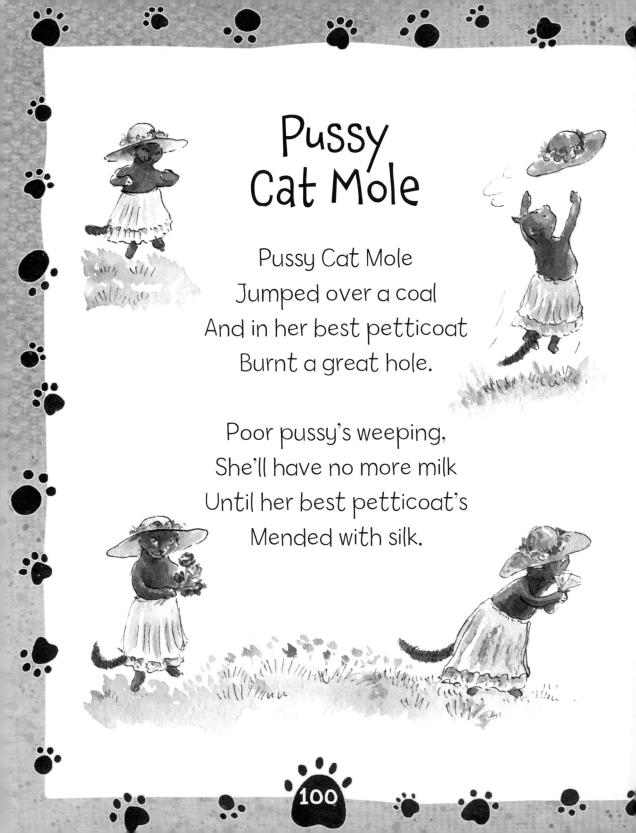

High in the Pine Tree

High in the pine tree,
The little turtledove
Made a little nursery
To please her little love.

"Coo," said the turtledove,
"Coo," said she,
In the long shady branches
Of the dark pine tree.

Where, O Where

Where, O where,
Has my little dog gone?
O where, O where, can he be?
With his tail cut short,
And his ears cut long,
O where, O where, has he gone?

I Love Little Pussy

I love little pussy,
Her coat is so warm,
And if I don't hurt her,
She'll do me no harm.

So I'll not pull her tail,
Nor drive her away,
But pussy and I,
Very gently will play.

I'll sit by the fire,
And give her some food;
And pussy will love me
Because I am good.

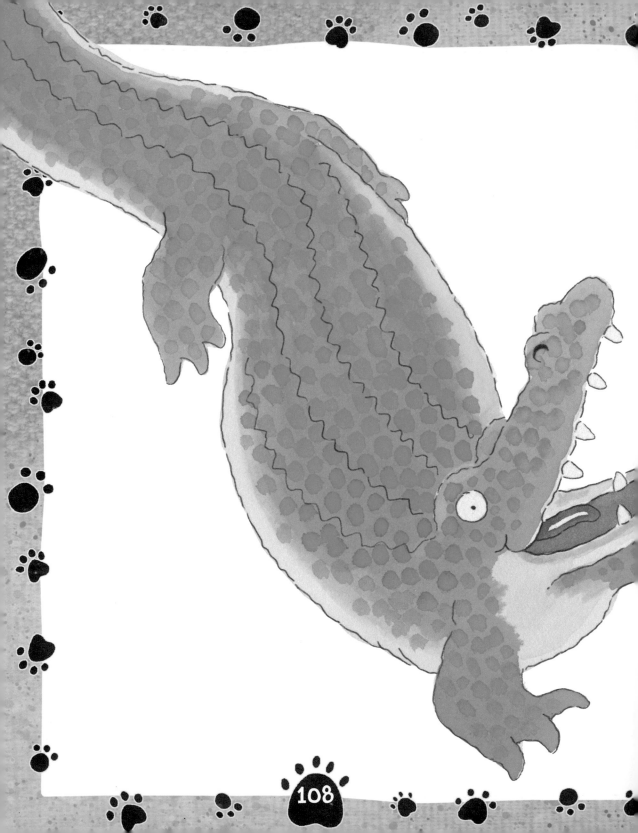

The Crocodile

If you should meet a crocodile
Don't take a stick and poke him;
Ignore the welcome in his smile,
Be careful not to stroke him.

For as he sleeps upon the Nile,
He thinner gets and thinner;
So whene'er you meet a crocodile
He's ready for his dinner.

Christine F Fletcher

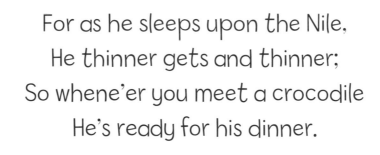

Who Killed Cock Robin?

Who killed Cock Robin?
"I," said the Sparrow,
"With my bow and arrow,
I killed Cock Robin."

Who saw him die?
"I," said the Fly,
"With my little eye,
I saw him die."

Who caught his blood?
"I," said the Fish,
"With my little dish,
I caught his blood."

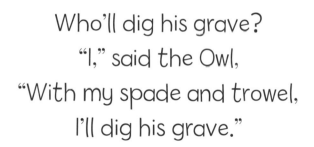

Who'll dig his grave?
"I," said the Owl,
"With my spade and trowel,
I'll dig his grave."

Who'll be the clerk?
"I," said the Lark,
"If it's not in the dark,
I'll be the clerk."

Who'll be the parson?
"I," said the Rook,
"With my little book,
I'll be the parson."

Who'll sing a psalm?
"I," said the Thrush,
As she sat on a bush,
"I'll sing a psalm."

Who'll be chief mourner?
"I," said the Dove,
"I mourn for my love,
I'll be chief mourner."

Who'll toll the bell?
"I," said the Bull,
"Because I can pull,
I'll toll the bell."

All the birds of the air
Fell sighing and sobbing,
When they heard the bell toll
For poor Cock Robin.

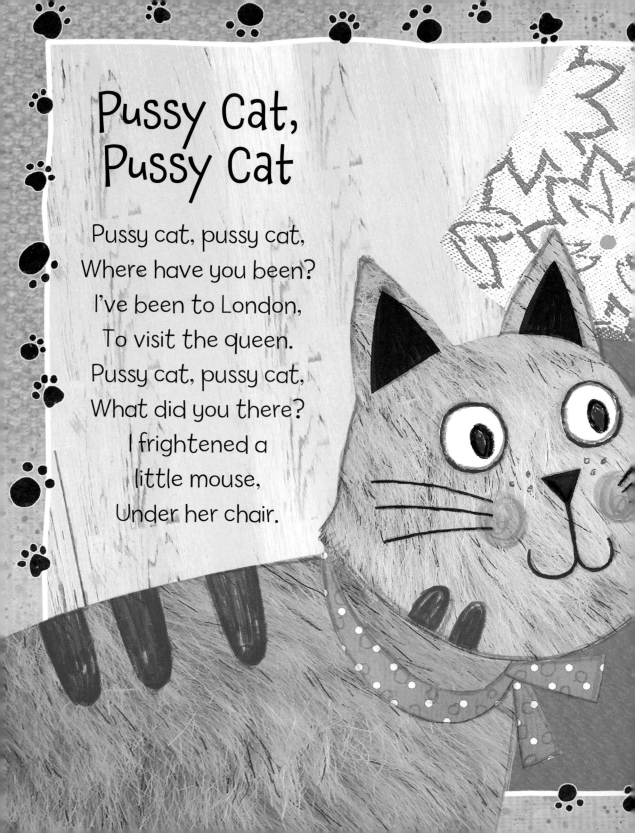

Pussy Cat,
Pussy Cat

Pussy cat, pussy cat,
Where have you been?
I've been to London,
To visit the queen.
Pussy cat, pussy cat,
What did you there?
I frightened a
little mouse,
Under her chair.

The Hobby-horse

I had a little hobby-horse,
And it was dapple grey;
Its head was made of pea-straw,
Its tail was made of hay.

I sold it to an old woman
For a copper groat;
And I'll not sing my song again
Without another coat.

The Lion and the Unicorn

The lion and the unicorn
Were fighting for the crown;
The lion beat the unicorn
All around the town.

Some gave them white bread
And some gave them brown;
Some gave them plum cake
And drummed them out of town!

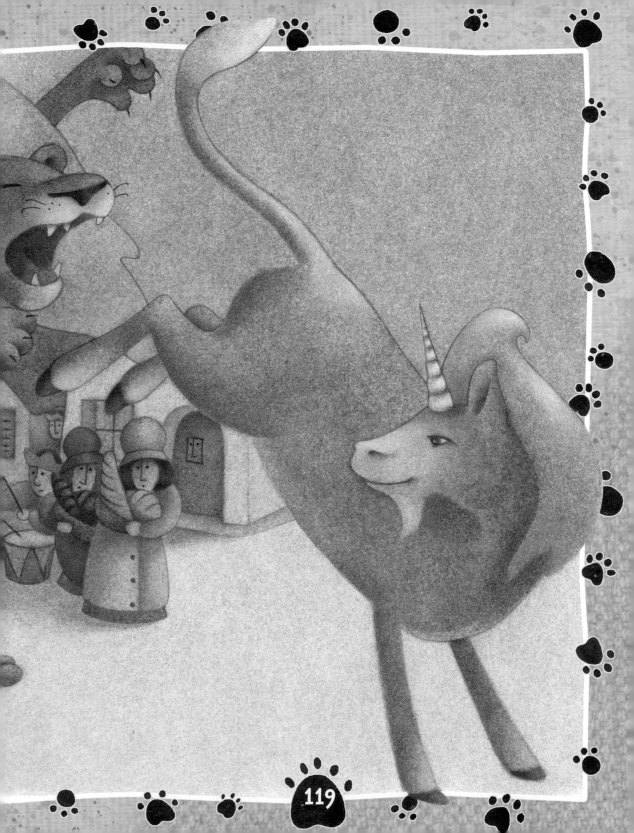

The Little Turtle

There was a little turtle,
He lived in a box.
He swam in a puddle,
He climbed on the rocks.

He snapped at a mosquito,
He snapped at a flea.
He snapped at a minnow,
And he snapped at me.

He caught the mosquito,
He caught the flea.
He caught the minnow,
But he didn't catch me.

Vachel Lindsay
1879–1931, b. USA

Ding, Dong, Bell

Ding, dong, bell,
Pussy's in the well.

Who put her in?
Little Johnny Flynn.

Who pulled her out?
Little Tommy Stout.

What a naughty boy was that
To try to drown poor pussy cat,

Who never did him any harm,
But killed the mice in the farmer's barn.

Gently down the stream

PLAYING TOGETHER

Beep, beep, beep! Beep, beep, beep!

One potato, Two potato

Ring-a-ring o' Roses

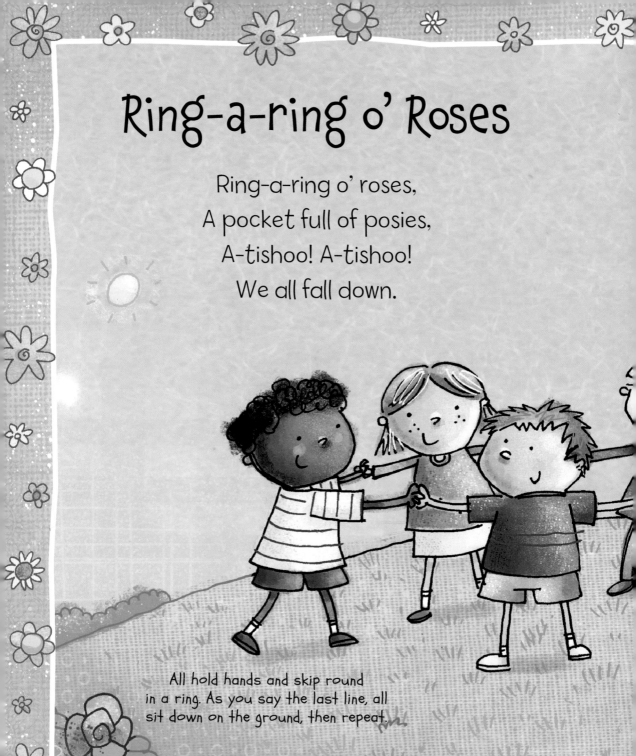

Ring-a-ring o' roses,
A pocket full of posies,
A-tishoo! A-tishoo!
We all fall down.

All hold hands and skip round
in a ring. As you say the last line, all
sit down on the ground, then repeat.

The king has sent his daughter,
To fetch a pail of water,
A-tishoo! A-tishoo!
We all fall down.

The bird upon the steeple,
Sits high above the people,
A-tishoo! A-tishoo!
We all fall down.

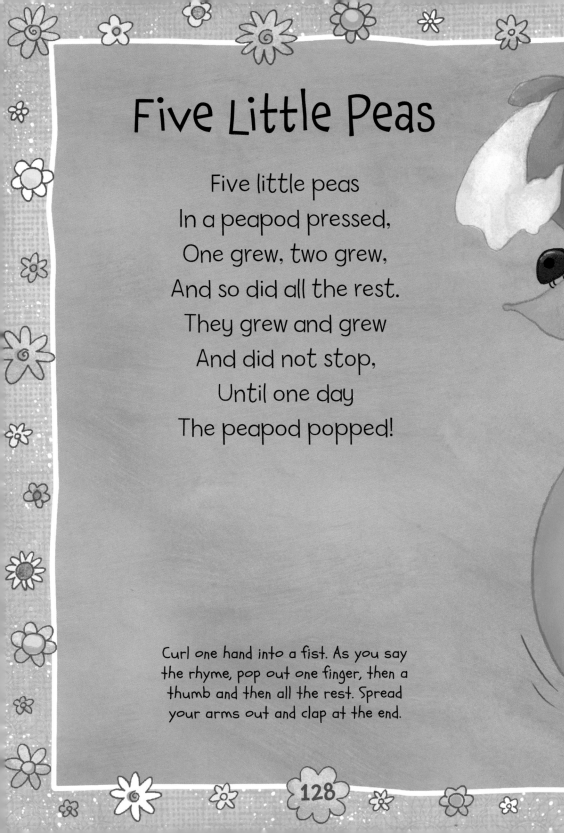

Five Little Peas

Five little peas
In a peapod pressed,
One grew, two grew,
And so did all the rest.
They grew and grew
And did not stop,
Until one day
The peapod popped!

Curl one hand into a fist. As you say
the rhyme, pop out one finger, then a
thumb and then all the rest. Spread
your arms out and clap at the end.

If you're Happy and you Know it

If you're happy and you know it,
clap your hands.
If you're happy and you know it,
clap your hands.
If you're happy and you know it
and you really want to show it,
If you're happy and you know it,
clap your hands.

Clap your hands when you get to those words in the rhyme.

Stamp your feet when you get to those words in the rhyme, then nod your head when you reach the third verse.

If you're happy and you know it,
stamp your feet.
If you're happy and you know it,
stamp your feet.
If you're happy and you know it
and you really want to show it,
If you're happy and you know it,
stamp your feet.

If you're happy and you know it,
nod your head.
If you're happy and you know it,
nod your head.
If you're happy and you know it
and you really want to show it,
If you're happy and you know it,
nod your head.

Row, Row, Row your Boat

Row, row, row your boat,
Gently down the stream.
Merrily, merrily, merrily, merrily,
Life is but a dream.

Row, row, row your boat,
Gently down the stream.
If you see a crocodile,
Don't forget to scream!

Row, row, row your boat,
Gently to the shore.
If you see a lion,
Don't forget to roar!

Sit across from your
partner, holding hands and
rocking back and forth.
Scream on the second verse!
Roar on the third verse!

Round and Round the Garden

Round and round the garden
Like a teddy bear,
One step, two step,
Tickle you under there!

Draw circles with your finger around
the palm. Walk your fingers up the arm
in two steps. Tickle under the arm!

One Potato

One potato,
Two potato,
Three potato,
Four,
Five potato,
Six potato,
Seven potato more.

Take turns with your partner in placing one fist on top of another to build a tower.

When you reach seven start again.

139

I'm a Little Teapot

I'm a little teapot,
Short and stout,
Here's my handle,
Here's my spout.

When I see the teacups,
Hear me shout,
"Tip me up, and pour me out!"

Place one hand on your
hip to be the handle.

Place the other arm out to
the side to be the spout.

On the final line, lean over to
one side to pour the tea.

Head and Shoulders, Knees and Toes

Head and shoulders, knees and toes,
Knees and toes,

142

Head and shoulders, knees and toes,
Knees and toes,

And eyes and ears and mouth and nose,

Head and shoulders, knees and toes,
Knees and toes.

Touch each part of
the body as you
sing the rhyme.

One, Two, Three, Four, Five

One, two, three, four, five,
Once I caught a fish alive;
Six, seven, eight, nine, ten,
Then I let it go again.

Why did you let it go?
Because it bit my finger so.
Which finger did it bite?
This little finger on my right.

Count to five using your fingers on
one hand, then count to ten using the
other hand. Shake out both hands.

Pretend to bite, then wiggle your
little finger on the right hand.

This Little Pig

This little pig went to market;

Market

This little pig stayed at home;
This little pig had roast beef;
This little pig had none;

Read the first line and
wiggle the big toe.

Read the next line and wiggle
the next toe and so on. On
the final line, tickle the foot.

146

And this little pig cried,
"Wee-wee-wee-wee-wee!"
All the way home.

The Wheels on the Bus

The wheels on the bus
go round and round,
Round and round, round and round.
The wheels on the bus
go round and round,
All day long.
(Roll your hands over each other.)

The horn on the bus
goes beep, beep, beep!
Beep, beep, beep! Beep, beep, beep!
The horn on the bus
goes beep, beep, beep!
All day long.
(Pretend to honk the horn.)

The wipers on the bus go swish, swish, swish!
Swish, swish, swish! Swish, swish, swish!
The wipers on the bus go swish, swish, swish!
All day long.
(Swish your arms like windscreen wipers.)

The people on the bus bounce up and down,
Up and down, up and down.
The people on the bus
bounce up and down,
All day long.
(Bounce up and down.)

The mummies on the bus
go chatter, chatter, chatter,
Chatter, chatter, chatter!
Chatter, chatter, chatter!
The mummies on the bus
go chatter, chatter, chatter!
All day long.

(Open and close your fingers and thumb.)

Two Little Dicky birds

Two little dicky birds sitting on a wall;
One named Peter, one named Paul.
Fly away Peter, fly away Paul!
Come back Peter, come back Paul!

Use your index fingers
to be Peter and Paul.

Wiggle each finger in turn.

Next, put each finger behind
you as if to fly away.

On the last line, bring each
finger back in front of you.

I Hear Thunder

I hear thunder, I hear thunder,
Hark, don't you?
Hark, don't you?
Pitter patter raindrops,
Pitter patter raindrops,
I'm wet through,
So are you.

Crash!

Boom!

Cup one hand to your ear.
Use both hands to wiggle
fingers like rain drops.
Shake your hands as if
you're drying them.

156

TASTY TREATS

Kissed the girls and made them cry

They licked the platter clean

The Queen of Hearts

The Queen of Hearts,
She made some tarts,
All on a summer's day;
The Knave of Hearts,
He stole the tarts,
And took them clean away.

The King of Hearts
Called for the tarts,
And beat the Knave full sore;
The Knave of Hearts
Brought back the tarts,
And vowed he'd steal no more.

Peter Piper

Peter Piper picked
a peck of pickled peppers;

A peck of pickled peppers
Peter Piper picked.

If Peter Piper picked
a peck of pickled peppers,

Where's the peck
of pickled peppers
Peter Piper picked?

161

Georgie Porgie

Georgie Porgie, pudding and pie,
Kissed the girls and made them cry;
When the boys came out to play,
Georgie Porgie ran away.

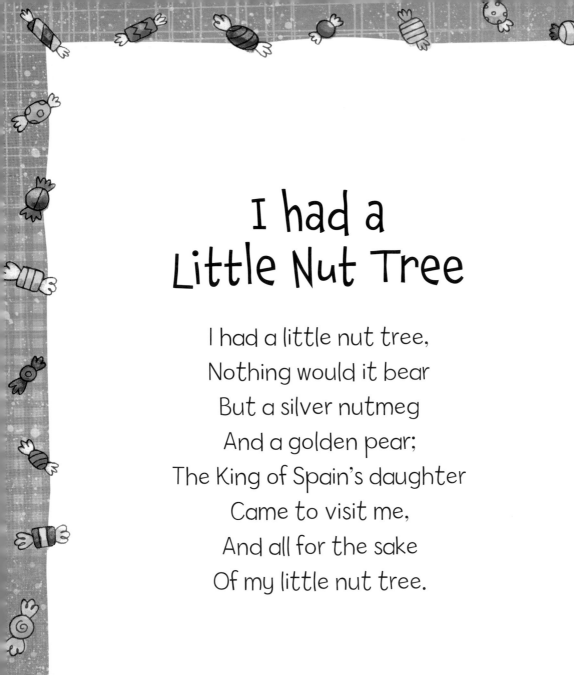

I had a
Little Nut Tree

I had a little nut tree,
Nothing would it bear
But a silver nutmeg
And a golden pear;
The King of Spain's daughter
Came to visit me,
And all for the sake
Of my little nut tree.

Peter, Peter

Peter, Peter, pumpkin eater,
Had a wife and couldn't keep her!
He put her in a pumpkin shell,
And there he kept her very well!

Mix a Pancake

Mix a pancake,
Stir a pancake,
Pop it in the pan;

Fry the pancake;
Toss the pancake,
Catch it if you can.

Christina Rossetti
1830–94, b. England

169

Little Jack Horner

Little Jack Horner
Sat in the corner,
Eating his Christmas pie;
He put in a thumb,
And pulled out a plum,
And said, "What a good boy am I."

I always Eat my Peas with Honey

I always eat my peas with honey;
I've done it all my life.
It makes the peas taste kind of funny
But it keeps them on the knife.

Anonymous

173

Simple Simon

Simple Simon met a pieman
Going to the fair;
Says Simple Simon to the pieman,
"Let me taste your ware."

Says the pieman to Simple Simon,
"Show me first your penny."
Says Simple Simon to the pieman,
"Sir, I haven't any."

Old Mother Hubbard

Old Mother Hubbard
Went to the cupboard,
To get her poor dog a bone.
But when she got there
The cupboard was bare,
And so the poor dog had none.

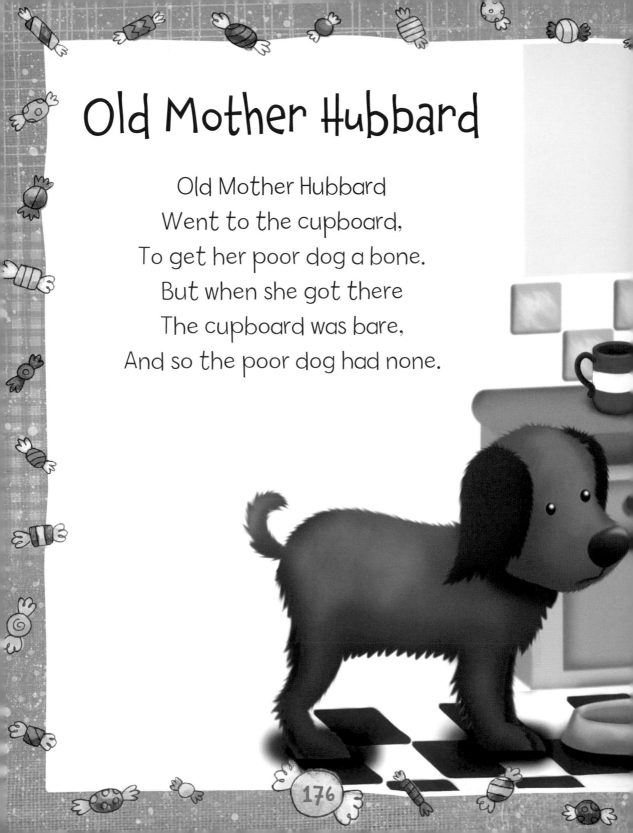

What are Little Boys made of?

What are little boys made of?
Frogs and snails, and puppy dogs' tails,
That's what little boys are made of.

What are little girls made of?
Sugar and spice, and all things nice,
That's what little girls are made of.

Little Tommy Tucker

Little Tommy Tucker
Sings for his supper.

What shall we give him?
White bread and butter.

How shall he cut it
Without a knife?

How will he be married
Without a wife?

Pease Porridge Hot

Pease porridge hot,
Pease porridge cold,
Pease porridge in the pot,
Nine days old.

Some like it hot,
Some like it cold,
Some like it in the pot,
Nine days old!

Oranges and Lemons

"Oranges and lemons",
Say the bells of St Clement's.

"You owe me five farthings",
Say the bells of St Martin's.

"When will you pay me?"
Say the bells of Old Bailey.

"When I grow rich,"
Say the bells of Shoreditch.

"When will that be?"
Say the bells of Stepney.

"I do not know,"
Says the great bell of Bow.

Here comes a candle to light you to bed.
Here comes a chopper to chop off your head!

Tom, Tom
the Piper's Son

Tom, Tom, the piper's son,
Stole a pig, and away did run,
The pig was eat,
And Tom was beat,
And Tom went howling
Down the street.

Jack Sprat

Jack Sprat could eat no fat,
His wife could eat no lean,
So between them both, you see,
They licked the platter clean.

Jack ate all the lean,
Joan ate all the fat,
The bone they picked it clean,
Then gave it to the cat.

The Muffin Man

O, do you know the muffin man,
The muffin man, the muffin man,
O, do you know the muffin man,
Who lives in Drury Lane?

O yes, I know the muffin man,
The muffin man, the muffin man,
O yes, I know the muffin man,
Who lives in Drury Lane.

I saw three ships
come sailing by

OUT AND ABOUT

Up and down the City Road,
In and out The Eagle

He'll come back and marry me

Rub-a-dub-dub

Rub-a-dub-dub,
Three men in a tub,
And who do you think they be?
The butcher, the baker,
The candlestick maker,
And all of them going to sea.

Pop goes the weasel

Half a pound of tuppenny rice,
Half a pound of treacle,
That's the way the money goes,
Pop goes the weasel!

Up and down the City Road,
In and out The Eagle,
That's the way the money goes,
Pop goes the weasel!

Every night when I go out
The monkey's on the table,
Take a stick and knock it off,
Pop goes the weasel!

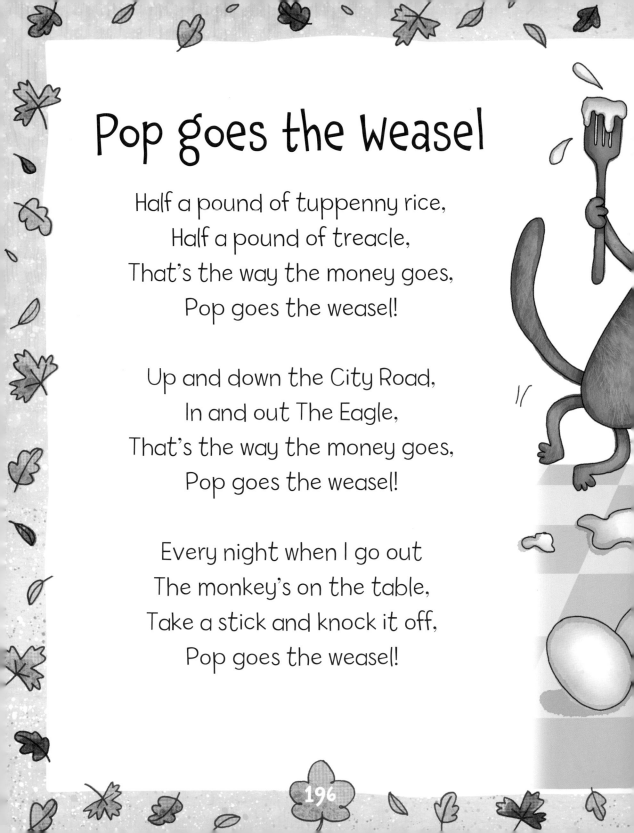

Bobby Shaftoe

Bobby Shaftoe's gone to sea,
Silver buckles on his knee;
He'll come back and marry me,
Bonny Bobby Shaftoe!

Bobby Shaftoe's young and fair,
Combing down his yellow hair;
He's my love for evermore,
Bonny Bobby Shaftoe!

This is the Way

This is the way the ladies ride,
Tri, tre, tre, tree,
Tri, tre, tre, tree,
This is the way the ladies ride,
Tri, tre, tre, tre, tri-tre-tre-tree!

This is the way
the gentlemen ride,
Gallop-a-trip,
Gallop-a-trot,
This is the way
the gentlemen ride,
Gallop-a-gallop-a-trot!

This is the way the farmers ride,
Hobbledy-hoy,
Hobbledy-hoy;
This is the way the farmers ride,
Hobbledy, hobbledy-hoy!

Ladybird, Ladybird

Ladybird, ladybird fly away home,
Your house is on fire
And your children are gone,
All except one and that's little Ann,
For she crept under the frying pan.

As I was going to St Ives

As I was going to St Ives,
I met a man with seven wives.
Each wife had seven sacks,
Each sack had seven cats,
Each cat had seven kits;
Kits, cats, sacks and wives,
How many were going to St Ives?

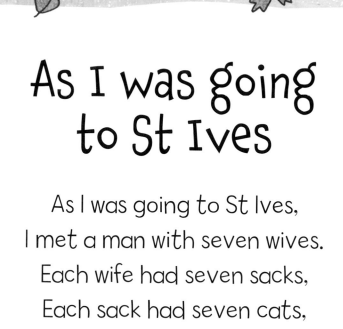

If all the World were Paper

If all the world were paper,
And all the sea were ink,
If all the trees were bread and cheese,
What should we have to drink?

To Market, to Market

To market, to market
to buy a fat pig;
Home again, home again,
jiggety-jig.

To market, to market
to buy a fat hog;
Home again, home again,
jiggety-jog.

Yankee Doodle

Yankee Doodle came to town,
Riding on a pony;
He stuck a feather in his cap
And called it macaroni.

Yankee doodle, doodle do,
Yankee doodle dandy,
All the lasses are so smart,
And sweet as sugar candy.

I Saw Three Ships

I saw three ships come sailing by,
Sailing by, sailing by,
I saw three ships come sailing by,
On New Year's Day in the morning.

And what do you think
was in them then,
In them then,
in them then?
And what do you think
was in them then,
On New Year's Day in
the morning?

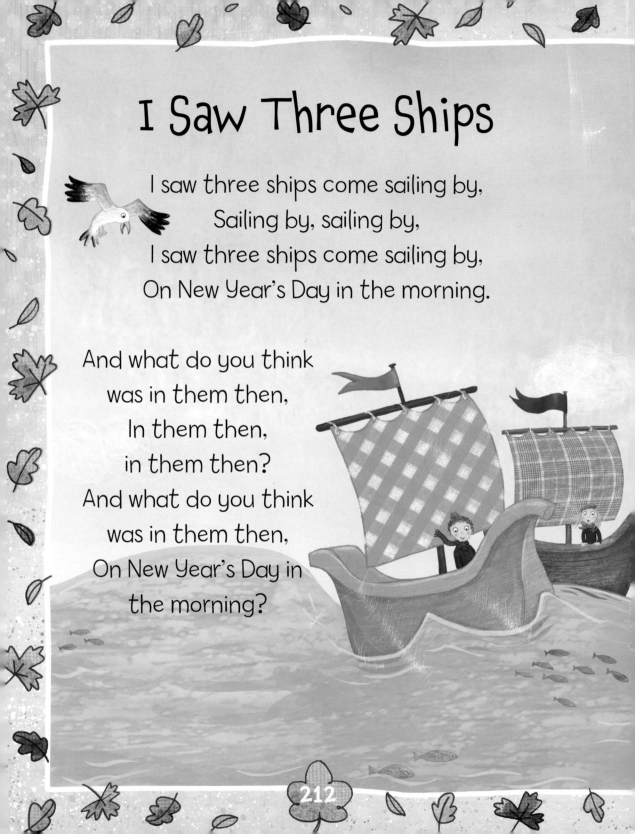

Three pretty girls were in them then,
In them then, in them then,
Three pretty girls were in them then,
On New Year's Day in the morning.

How many Miles to Babylon?

How many miles to Babylon?
Three score miles and ten.
Can I get there by candlelight?
Aye, and back again.
If your feet are nimble and light,
You may get there by candlelight.

As I was Going Out

As I was going out one day
My head fell off and rolled away,
But when I saw that it was gone,
I picked it up and put it on.

And when I got into the street
A fellow cried, "Look at your feet!"
I looked at them and sadly said,
"I've left both asleep in bed!"

Ride a Cock Horse

Ride a cock horse
To Banbury Cross,
To see a fine lady
Upon a white horse.
With rings on her fingers
And bells on her toes,
She shall have music
Wherever she goes.

London Bridge is Falling Down

London Bridge is falling down,
Falling down, falling down,
London Bridge is falling down,
My fair lady.

Build it up with wood and clay,
Wood and clay, wood and clay,
Build it up with wood and clay,
My fair lady.

Wood and clay will wash away,
Wash away, wash away,
Wood and clay will wash away,
My fair lady.

If all the Seas were One Sea

If all the seas were one sea,
What a great sea that would be!
If all the trees were one tree,
What a great tree that would be!

If all the axes were one axe,
What a great axe that would be!
If all the men were one man,
What a great man that would be!

And if the great man took the great axe
And cut down the great tree,
And let it fall into the great sea,
What a great splish-splash that would be!

NUMBER RHYMES

Four-and-twenty blackbirds

Six little mice
sat down to spin

225

Five Little Ducks

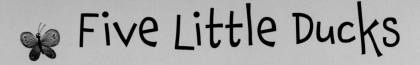

Five little ducks went swimming one day,
Over the hill and far away.
Mother duck said,
"Quack, quack, quack, quack!"
But only four little ducks came back.

Four little ducks went swimming one day,
Over the hill and far away.
Mother duck said,
"Quack, quack, quack, quack!"
But only three little ducks came back.

Three little ducks went swimming one day,
Over the hill and far away.
Mother duck said,
"Quack, quack, quack, quack!"
But only two little ducks came back.

Two little ducks went swimming one day,
Over the hill and far away.
Mother duck said,
"Quack, quack, quack, quack!"
But only one little duck came back.

One little duck went swimming one day,
Over the hill and far away.
Mother duck said,
"Quack, quack, quack, quack!"
And all her five little ducks came back!

One, Two, Three, Four

One, two, three, four,
Mary at the kitchen door.
Five, six, seven, eight,
Eating cherries off a plate.

Sing a Song of Sixpence

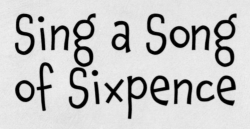

Sing a song of sixpence,
A pocket full of rye;
Four-and-twenty blackbirds
Baked in a pie.

When the pie was opened,
The birds began to sing;
Wasn't that a dainty dish
To set before the king?

The king was in his counting house,
Counting out his money;
The queen was in the parlour
Eating bread and honey.

The maid was in the garden
Hanging out the clothes,
When down came a blackbird,
And pecked off her nose.

One, Two, Buckle my Shoe

One, two,
buckle my shoe;

Three, four,
knock at
the door;

Five, six, pick up sticks;

Seven, eight, lay them straight;

Nine, ten,
a big fat hen.

Six Little Mice

Six little mice sat down to spin;
Pussy passed by and she peeped in.
"What are you doing, my little men?"
"Weaving coats for gentlemen."
"Shall I come in and cut off your threads?"
"No, no, Mistress Pussy, you'd bite off our heads."
"Oh, no, I'll not, I'll help you to spin."
"That may be so, but you don't come in!"

Hot Cross Buns!

Hot cross buns! Hot cross buns!
One a penny, two a penny,
Hot cross buns!

Give them to your daughters,
Give them to your sons,
One a penny, two a penny,
Hot cross buns!

Three Little Kittens

Three little kittens, they lost their mittens,
And they began to cry,
"Oh, Mother dear, we sadly fear,
That we have lost our mittens."
"What! Lost your mittens,
you naughty kittens!
Then you shall have no pie.
Mee-ow, mee-ow, mee-ow.
Then you shall have no pie."

Three little kittens, they found their mittens,
And they began to cry,
"Oh, mother dear, see here, see here,
For we have found our mittens."
"Put on your mittens, you silly kittens!
And you shall have some pie."

Hickety Pickety

Hickety pickety, my black hen,
She lays eggs for gentlemen.
Sometimes nine and sometimes ten,
Hickety pickety, my black hen.

Two Cats of Kilkenny

There once were two cats of Kilkenny,
Each thought there was one cat too many,
So they fought and they fit,
And they scratched and they bit,
Till, excepting their nails
And the tips of their tails,
Instead of two cats, there weren't any.

One for Sorrow

One for sorrow,
Two for joy,
Three for a girl,
Four for a boy.
Five for silver,
Six for gold,

Seven for a secret,
Never to be told.
Eight for a wish,
Nine for a kiss,
Ten for a bird you
want to miss.

Three Blind Mice

Three blind mice, three blind mice,
See how they run! See how they run!
They all ran after the farmer's wife
Who cut off their tails
with a carving knife;
Did you ever see
such a thing in your life
As three blind mice?

I Love Sixpence

I love sixpence, pretty little sixpence,
I love sixpence better than my life;
I spent a penny of it, I spent another,
And I took fourpence home to my wife.

Oh, my little fourpence,
pretty little fourpence,
I love fourpence better than my life;
I spent a penny of it, I spent another,
And I took twopence home to my wife.

Oh, my little twopence,
pretty little twopence,
I love twopence better than my life;
I spent a penny of it, I spent another,
And I took nothing home to my wife.

Five Little Pussy Cats

Five little pussy cats playing near the door;
One ran and hid inside
And then there
were four.

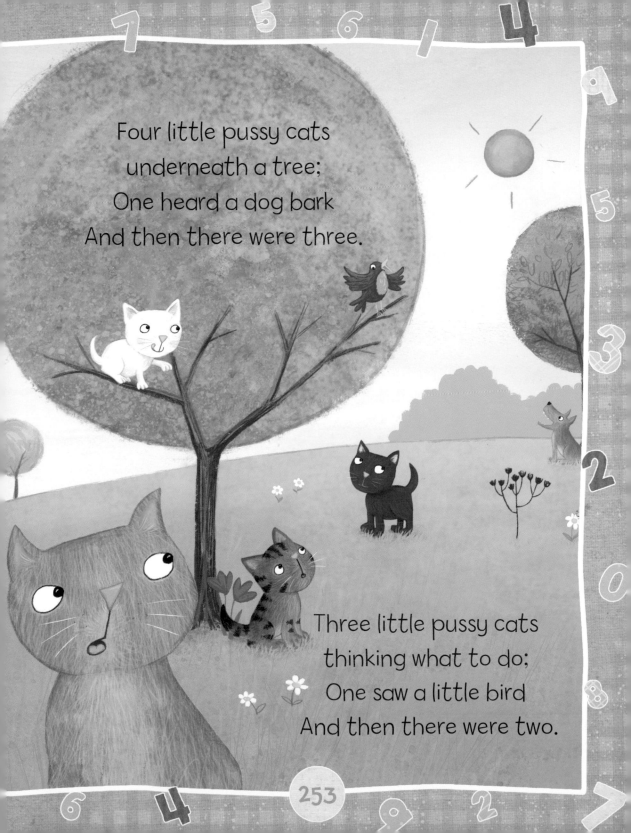

Four little pussy cats
underneath a tree;
One heard a dog bark
And then there were three.

Three little pussy cats
thinking what to do;
One saw a little bird
And then there were two.

Two little pussy cats sitting in the sun;
One ran to catch his tail
And then there was one.

One little pussy cat looking for some fun;
He saw a butterfly
And then there was none.

It rains on the umbrellas here

WHATEVER THE WEATHER

The wind is passing through

And we shall have snow

Incy Wincy Spider

Incy Wincy Spider
Climbed up the water spout;
Down came the rain
And washed the spider out.

Out came the sun
And dried up all the rain;
So Incy Wincy Spider
Climbed up the spout again.

The Mulberry Bush

Here we go round the mulberry bush,
The mulberry bush, the mulberry bush,
Here we go round the mulberry bush,
On a cold and frosty morning.

This is the way we wash our hands,
Wash our hands, wash our hands,
This is the way we wash our hands,
On a cold and frosty morning.

This is the way we brush our hair,
Brush our hair, brush our hair,
This is the way we brush our hair,
On a cold and frosty morning.

This is the way we go to school,
Go to school, go to school,
This is the way we go to school,
On a cold and frosty morning.

This is the way we wave goodbye,
Wave goodbye, wave goodbye,
This is the way we wave goodbye,
On a cold and frosty morning.

It's Raining

It's raining, it's pouring,
The old man is snoring;
He went to bed
And bumped his head
And couldn't get up in the morning!

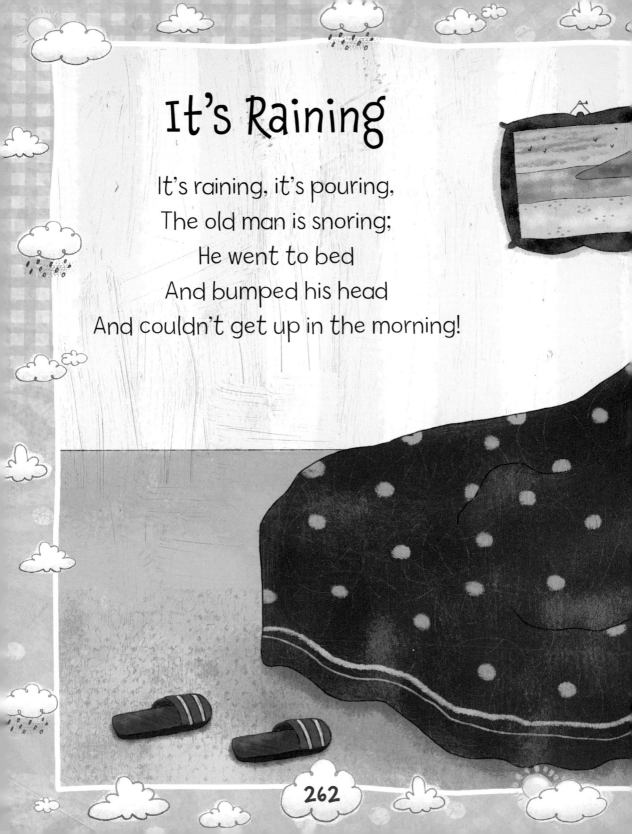

Blow, Wind, Blow

Blow, wind, blow,
And go, mill, go;
That the miller
May grind his corn;
That the baker may take it,
And into bread make it,
And bring us some
Hot in the morn.

Doctor Foster

Doctor Foster
Went to Gloucester
In a shower of rain.
He stepped in a puddle
Right up to his middle
And never went there again!

The Twelve Months

Snowy,

Flowy,

Blowy,

Showery,

Flowery,

Bowery,

Hoppy,
   Croppy,
      Droppy,

Breezy,
   Sneezy,
      Freezy.

George Ellis
1753–1815, b. England

Rain

Rain on the green grass,
Rain on the trees,
Rain on the rooftop,
But not on me!

The North Wind doth Blow

The north wind doth blow,
And we shall have snow,
And what will poor robin do then,
Poor thing?

He'll sit in a barn,
And keep himself warm,
And hide his head under his wing,
Poor thing.

Whether the Weather

Whether the weather be fine,
Or whether the weather be not,
Whether the weather be cold,
Or whether the weather be hot,
We'll weather the weather
Whatever the weather,
Whether we like it or not!

First Day of May

The fair maid who, the first of May,
Goes to the fields at break of day,
And washes in dew from the hawthorn tree,
Will ever after handsome be.

Rain

The rain is falling all around,
It falls on field and tree,
It rains on the umbrellas here,
And on the ships at sea.

Robert Louis Stevenson
1850–94, b. Scotland

279

Who has seen the Wind?

Who has seen the wind?
Neither I nor you:
But when the leaves hang trembling,
The wind is passing through.

Who has seen the wind?
Neither you nor I:
But when the trees bow down their heads,
The wind is passing by.

Christina Rossetti
1830–94, b. England

Over the Hills

Tom, he was a piper's son,
He learned to play when he was young,
And all the tunes that he could play
Was, "Over the hills and far away".
Over the hills and a great way off,
The wind shall blow my top-knot off.

Rain, Rain

Rain, rain, go away,
Come again another day.

Rain, rain, go away,
Little Johnny wants to play.

Red Sky at Night

Red sky at night,
Shepherd's delight;
Red sky in the morning,
Shepherd's warning.

upstairs and downstairs
In his night gown

BEDTIME RHYMES

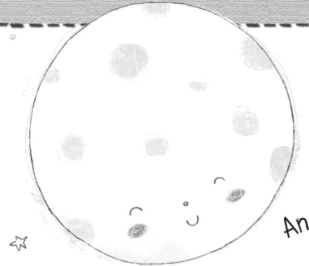

I see the moon
And the moon sees me

up above the world so high

Twinkle, Twinkle, Little Star

Twinkle, twinkle, little star,
How I wonder what you are.
Up above the world so high,
Like a diamond in the sky.

When the blazing sun is gone,
When he nothing shines upon,
Then you show your little light,
Twinkle, twinkle, all the night.

Then the traveller in the dark,
Thanks you for your tiny spark.
He could not see which way to go,
If you did not twinkle so.

In the dark blue sky you keep,
And often through my curtains peep.
For you never shut your eye,
Till the sun is in the sky.

Rock-a-bye, Baby

Rock-a-bye, baby,
On the tree-top,
When the wind blows,
The cradle will rock.

When the bough breaks,
The cradle will fall.
And down will come baby,
Cradle and all.

Come, let's to Bed

Come, let's to bed, says Sleepy-head;
Sit up awhile, says Slow;
Bang on the pot, says Greedy-gut,
We'll sup before we go.

To bed, to bed, cried Sleepy-head,
But all the rest said No!
It is morning now,
You must milk the cow,
And tomorrow to bed we go.

The Evening is Coming

The evening is coming,
The sun sinks to rest,
The birds are all flying
Straight home to the nest.

"Caw," says the crow
As he flies overhead,
"It's time little children
Were going to bed!"

Sleep, Baby, Sleep

Sleep, baby, sleep,
Thy father guards the sheep;
Thy mother shakes the dreamland tree
And from it fall sweet dreams for thee,
Sleep, baby, sleep.

Sleep, baby, sleep,
Our cottage vale is deep;
The little lamb is on the green,
The woolly fleece so soft and clean,
Sleep, baby, sleep.

Sleep, baby, sleep,
Down where the woodbines creep;
Be always like the lamb so mild,
A kind and sweet and gentle child,
Sleep, baby, sleep.

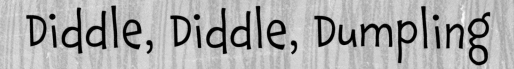

Diddle, Diddle, Dumpling

Diddle, diddle, dumpling, my son John,
Went to bed with his trousers on;
One shoe off, and one shoe on,
Diddle, diddle, dumpling, my son John.

I See the Moon

I see the moon,
And the moon sees me;
God bless the moon,
And God bless me!

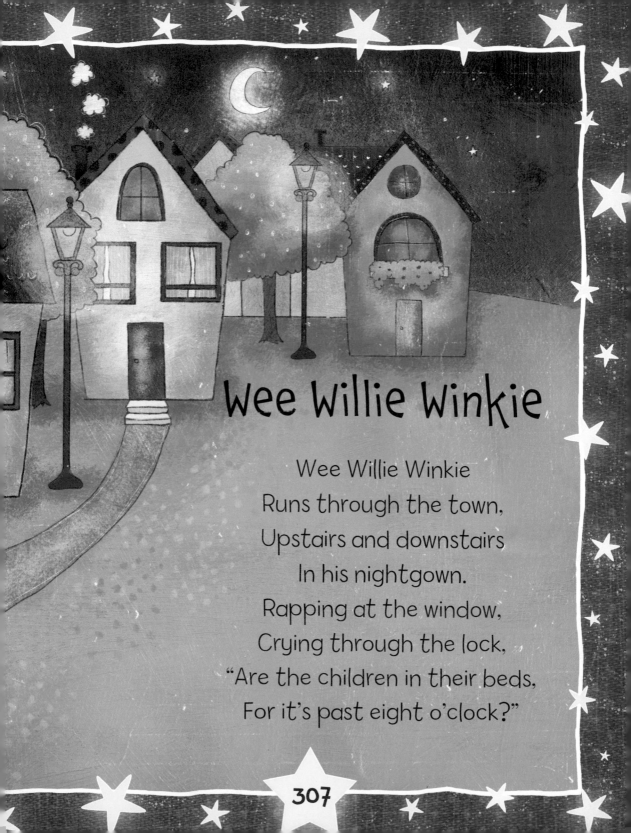

Wee Willie Winkie

Wee Willie Winkie
Runs through the town,
Upstairs and downstairs
In his nightgown.
Rapping at the window,
Crying through the lock,
"Are the children in their beds,
For it's past eight o'clock?"

Teddy Bear, Teddy Bear

Teddy bear, teddy bear, touch the ground.
Teddy bear, teddy bear, turn around.
Teddy bear, teddy bear, show your shoe.
Teddy bear, teddy bear, that will do.

Teddy bear, teddy bear, run upstairs.
Teddy bear, teddy bear, say your prayers.
Teddy bear, teddy bear, blow out the light.
Teddy bear, teddy bear, say goodnight.

Hush, Little Baby

Hush, little baby, don't say a word,
Papa's going to buy you a mocking bird.

If the mocking bird won't sing,
Papa's going to buy you a diamond ring.

If the diamond ring turns to brass,
Papa's going to buy you a looking-glass.

If the looking-glass gets broke,
Papa's going to buy you a billy-goat.

If the billy-goat runs away,
Papa's going to buy you another today.

Girls and Boys, Come Out to Play

Girls and boys, come out to play,
The moon doth shine as bright as day;
Leave your supper, and leave your sleep,
And come with your playfellows into
the street.

Come with a whoop, come with a call,
Come with a good will or not at all;
Up the ladder and down the wall,
A half-penny roll will serve us all.

313

A Candle, a Candle

A candle, a candle to light me to bed;
A pillow, a pillow to tuck up my head.
The moon is as sleepy as sleepy can be,
The stars are all pointing their fingers at me.

And Missus Hop-Robin, way up in her nest,
Is rocking her tired little babies to rest.
So give me a blanket to tuck up my toes,
And a little soft pillow to snuggle my nose.

Star Light, Star Bright

Star light, star bright,
First star I see tonight.
I wish I may,
I wish I might,
Have the wish
I wish tonight.

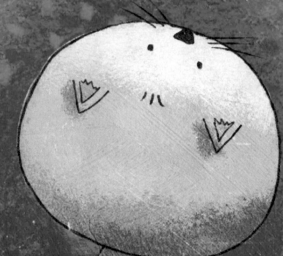

She saw a
glint of gold

STORY TIME

The mice were delighted

She placed one single pea right in the middle

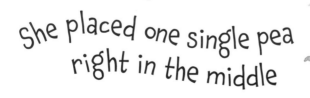

The Magic Porridge Pot

A Swedish folk tale

One day, just before Christmas, a poor farmer and his wife decided to sell their last cow.

They had no money left and no food. On the way to market, the farmer met a strange little man. He had a long white beard down to his bare toes and was wearing a huge black hat. He was carrying an old pot. "I shall give you this porridge pot in exchange for your cow!" declared the man. The farmer looked at the pot, then at his cow, and was about to say, 'Certainly not!' when a voice whispered, "Take me! Take me!"

Thinking the pot must be magic, the farmer agreed, and handed over the cow. As he picked up the porridge pot, the man vanished.

When the farmer explained what had happened to his wife she was very angry. Then the voice said, "Take me inside, clean me and polish me, and you shall see what you shall see!"

The farmer's wife was astonished. She did as she was told, but as she finished cleaning, the pot hopped off the table, and out of the door.

The farmer and his wife sat down by the fire, without saying a word. They had lost everything.

Down the road from the poor farmer, lived a rich, selfish man. His cook was in the kitchen making a huge Christmas pudding filled with sultanas, almonds and plums. The cook had just realised she didn't have a pot big enough for the pudding, when the old porridge pot trotted in.

"Goodness me!" she exclaimed. "The fairies must have sent you, just in time to take my pudding," and she poured in the ingredients.

As the last almond dropped to the bottom, the pot skipped out

of the door again. It trotted back
to the farmer and his wife, who
were delighted to discover the
wonderful pudding inside.

In the spring, the pot once more said to the farmer's wife, "Clean me, and polish me, and you shall see what you shall see."

The farmer's wife did as the pot said. As she finished, the pot hopped off the table, and out of the door.

Nearby, the rich man was counting his money. He was wondering where he could hide it, when in trotted the pot.

"Goodness me!" he exclaimed and filled the pot with his money. As he dropped in the last bag, the pot skipped out of the room.

The rich man shouted and hollered, but the pot trotted out of sight, down the road to the farmer's house.

The farmer and his wife were delighted to find bags of gold and silver in the pot. There was enough money to last them forever!

As for the porridge pot, it sat by the fire for many years. Then, one day, it trotted out of the door and was never, ever seen again.

The Princess and the Pea

A retelling from the original story by Hans Christian Andersen

The prince was very fed up. Everyone in the court seemed to think he should be married, but he insisted that his bride be a real, true and proper princess.

He had met plenty of nice girls who had come to the palace and said they were princesses. But, it seemed to the prince, either their manners were not exquisite enough, or their feet were too big.

The prince sat in the palace feeling glum, until one night there was a terrible storm. Rain lashed down, thunder rolled and lightning flashed.

Suddenly the door bell rang, and there, dripping wet, stood a girl. She said she was a princess, but she didn't look like one. Her hair was plastered to her head, her dress was wringing wet and her silk shoes were covered in mud. She was quite alone too.

The queen invited the girl in, but didn't believe for one moment that she was a princess.

While the girl sat sipping a mug of warm milk and honey, the queen supervised the making up of the bed in the second-best spare bedroom.

The queen told the maids to take off all the bedclothes and the mattress. Then she placed one single pea right in the middle of the bedstead. Next, the maids piled twenty mattresses on top of the pea, and then twenty feather quilts on top of the mattresses. And so the girl was shown to the room, and left for the night.

The next morning, the queen swept into the bedroom and asked the girl how she had slept.

"I didn't sleep a wink all night." said the girl. "There was a great, hard lump in the middle of the bed. It was quite dreadful. I am sure I am black and blue all over!"

Now everyone knew she really must be a princess, for only a real princess could be so soft-skinned.

The prince was delighted. They

were married at once, and lived very happily ever after. They always slept in very soft beds, and the pea was placed in the museum, where it probably still is today.

The Elves and the Shoemaker

A retelling from the original story by the Brothers Grimm

Once, there was a shoemaker and his wife. They worked very hard from morning till night. The shoes the shoemaker made were of the finest leather, but business was slow. One night he found he only had enough leather left for one more pair of shoes.

"Wife, I do not know what to do. I have just cut out the last piece of leather in the shop," he said sadly.

"Don't be too gloomy, husband," said his wife with a tired smile. "Perhaps you will be able to sell this last pair of shoes for a fine price."

The next day the shoemaker was

up early as usual. When he pulled back the shutters in the shop, he saw a fine pair of ladies' shoes already made! He put the shoes in the window of the shop, and before long a rich merchant came in and bought the shoes for his new wife.

The shoemaker was delighted, and bought enough leather to make two new pairs of shoes. The next day the same thing happened! He put the two new

pairs of shoes in the window, and
they sold straightaway.

This continued for many days.

The shoemaker would buy new leather, leave the pieces cut ready on his bench at night, and in the morning there would be the most exquisite shoes. Before long the shoemaker and his wife were no longer poor.

One day, the wife said, "Husband, I think we must see who has given us this good fortune so we may thank them."

The shoemaker agreed. So, he and his wife hid behind the door of the shop. As the town hall clock struck midnight, they heard the sound of tiny feet and little voices.

Two elves slid out from behind the skirting board and climbed onto the bench. They were soon hard at work, stitching away. The elves sang happily as they stitched. But their clothes were ragged and their feet looked frozen, as they had neither socks nor shoes.

Soon the leather was gone, and on the bench stood more shoes. The elves slipped away.

The next day, the shoemaker made two tiny pairs of boots. His wife set to work making two little pairs of red trousers and two

jackets with silver buttons and
knitted two little pairs of socks.
That night, they laid out the
clothes and boots,
and hid behind
the shop door.
As the town
hall clock struck
midnight, the
two little elves
appeared in
the workshop.

When they saw the gifts, they
clapped their hands in delight and
flung off their old rags. They tried
on their new clothes and boots,
and looked splendid. They slipped

behind the skirting board, and the shoemaker and his wife never saw the elves again.

But, once a year when the shoemaker opened his shop, on his bench he would find a pair of shoes. The stitching was so fine you would think it had been done by mice.

Goldilocks and the Three Bears

A retelling from the original tale by Andrew Lang

Once upon a time there was a little girl called Goldilocks, who lived in a forest with her parents.

Ever since she was tiny, her mother had told her not to wander off into the forest. But, one day, when her mother was busy in the kitchen, Goldilocks sneaked away.

For as long as she could remember, Goldilocks had longed to explore the forest. So, at first she was happy, looking at the wild flowers and listening to birds singing. But, it was not long before she become hopelessly lost.

Goldilocks wandered for hours and, as it grew darker, she became frightened. Suddenly, she saw a light from a little cottage.

She opened the door and looked

inside. On a wooden table there were three bowls of steaming hot porridge – a big one, a middle-sized one and a little one.

Goldilocks was so tired, she quite forgot her manners and sat down. The big bowl was too tall for her to reach. The middle-sized bowl was too hot. The little bowl was just right, so she ate it all up.

By the fire were three chairs —
a big one, a middle-sized one and a
little one. Goldilocks couldn't climb
onto the big one. The middle-sized
one was too hard. The little one
was just right, but as soon as she
sat down, it broke into pieces!

As Goldilocks scrambled to her
feet, she saw steps going upstairs.
There, she found three beds —

a big one, a middle-sized one and a little one. The big bed was much too hard. The middle-sized one was a bit soft. But, the little bed felt just right, so Goldilocks climbed in and fell fast asleep.

Now, the cottage belonged to three bears. When they arrived

home, they soon realized someone had been inside their cottage.

"Who has been eating my porridge?" growled Father Bear.

Mother Bear grumbled, "Who has been eating my porridge?"

And Baby Bear gasped, "Who has been eating my porridge, AND has eaten it all up?"

Next, the bears looked at their three chairs by the fire. They had all been moved around a bit.

Father Bear growled, "Who has been sitting on my chair?"

Mother Bear grumbled, "Who has been sitting on my chair?"

And Baby Bear gasped, "Who has been sitting on my chair, AND has broken it into bits?" Baby Bear began to cry.

Then, the bears went upstairs and looked into the bedroom.

Father Bear growled, "Who has been sleeping in my bed?"

Mother Bear grumbled, "Who has been sleeping in my bed?"

And Baby Bear gasped, "Who has been sleeping in my bed, AND is still there?"

Suddenly Goldilocks woke up. She saw the three very cross-looking bears staring at her and she was

very scared. She jumped off the
bed, ran downstairs and out of
the door. She ran all the way home
and the bears never saw her again.

The Town Mouse and the Country Mouse

An Aesop's Fable

Once upon a time, a town mouse went to see his cousin in the country. The mice were delighted to see each other, and the country mouse made the town mouse feel very welcome.

But the country mouse was very poor. He lived a simple life, in a barn

shared with other animals. He
was quite rough, with bad habits.
A plain meal of cheese and bread,
and a bed of straw were all he had

to offer the town mouse.

The town mouse was used to dining on fine food and sleeping in a soft bed. He turned up his nose

at the meal and lodgings the country mouse offered him.

"I cannot understand," he said to his country cousin, "how you can put up with such poor food, and sleep on straw. Come home with me and I'll show you how to live."

The country mouse was curious – after all, he had never seen the town. So, the two mice set off.

They arrived at the town mouse's residence late at night. It was a

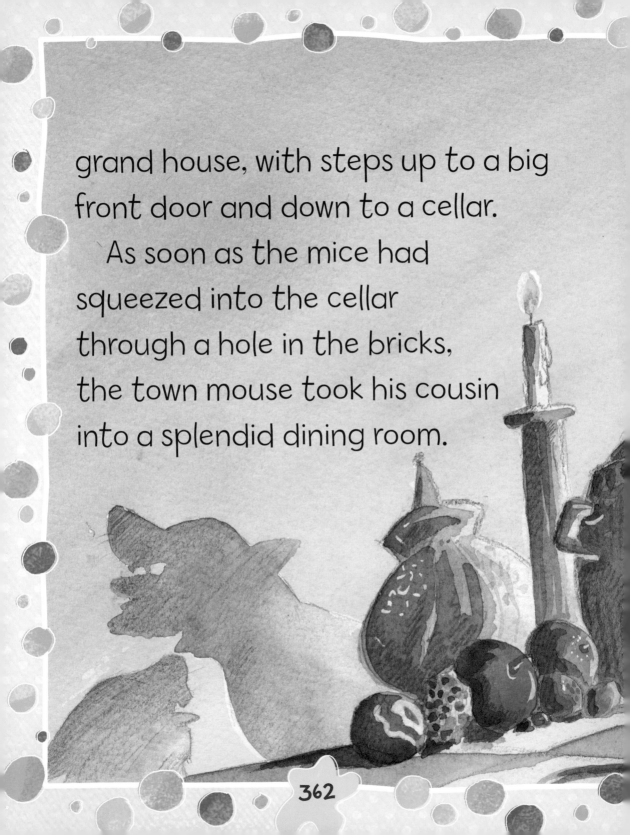

grand house, with steps up to a big front door and down to a cellar.

As soon as the mice had squeezed into the cellar through a hole in the bricks, the town mouse took his cousin into a splendid dining room.

There, they found the remains of a fine feast on the table, and were soon eating jellies and cakes.

Suddenly they heard a deep growling. "What is that?" asked the country mouse.

"It is only the dogs of the house," answered the town mouse.

"Only the dogs!" gasped the country mouse. "I don't like that kind of music at my dinner."

At that moment the door flew open, and in came two huge dogs. The two terrified mice quickly scampered down the table leg.

"Goodbye, town cousin," shouted the country mouse as he sprinted towards a little hole in the wall.

"Why cousin? Going so soon?"
asked the town mouse in surprise.
"Yes," replied the country mouse.
"Better bread and cheese in peace,
than jelly and cakes in fear."

The Boy Who Cried Wolf

An Aesop's Fable

There was once a shepherd boy who tended his sheep at the foot of a mountain, near a dark forest.

He was out on the slopes all day by himself, and he was often lonely and bored.

One day, the shepherd boy thought up a plan whereby he could get a little company and some excitement. He left his flock unattended and rushed down the slopes to the village. He pretended to be in a terrible panic he shouted, "Wolf! Wolf!" at the top of his voice.

The villagers came running to check he was unharmed. But when they realized there was no wolf, the villagers returned to their houses grumbling about the boy shouting false alarms.

A few days later the naughty boy tried the same trick again.

He ran down the mountainside screaming, "Wolf! Wolf!" Again the villagers came rushing to help him. This time the villagers were very angry when they realized the boy had managed to trick them again. Just a few days later, the shepherd boy was watching his flocks as usual. Suddenly, a wolf really

did come out of the forest!

Of course, the boy set off down the mountainside crying, "Wolf! Wolf!" even louder than before.

But the villagers, who had already been fooled twice,

thought the boy was deceiving them again. No one came to his aid, so the wolf made a good, tasty meal of the boy's whole flock.

Snow White and Rose Red

A retelling from the original story by the Brothers Grimm

Once upon a time there was a widow who lived with her two daughters. Snow White was quiet and gentle, while Rose Red was as wild as the hills.

One winter evening there was a knock at the door. Rose Red opened it, and gave a scream. There stood a big brown bear! In a deep rumbly voice the bear said, "Please don't be afraid. May I sleep by your fire? It is so cold outside."

The mother and girls agreed to let the bear stay. They fed him hot soup and brushed the snow from his fur. The bear stretched out by the fire, and was soon asleep.

In the morning, the bear left the cottage, but he returned every evening throughout the winter. Snow White, Rose Red and their mother became very fond of him.

When spring came, the bear told them he would not be returning.

"I have to guard my treasure. Once the snows melt all kinds of wicked people try to steal it," he said. He gave them all a hug and set off through the forest.

As he passed through the garden gate, the bear's fur caught on a nail. Snow White thought she saw a glint of gold, but the bear was gone.

A few days later, Rose Red and Snow White were in the woods when they saw a dwarf. His beard was trapped by a fallen tree.

"Don't stand there like a pair of silly geese! Help me!" he shrieked. They tried hard, but Rose Red and

Snow White couldn't lift the tree. So, Rose Red used her scissors to snip off the end of the beard.

The dwarf was furious. He snatched up a big bag of gold from the tree roots and disappeared without a word of thanks.

Some days later, the girls were walking by a stream when they saw the dwarf again. This time his beard was caught in his fishing line.

Again, the girls tried to untangle

him, but Snow White had to snip off another piece of his beard.

The dwarf was white with rage. He grasped a casket of jewels lying on the bank and stormed off without a word of thanks.

A few days later, the girls were on their way to the Spring Fair when they heard a terrible shrieking. The dwarf was struggling in the talons of an eagle. The girls tugged and tugged and the eagle let him go.

"You've torn my coat," muttered
the ungrateful dwarf. He picked up
a basket of pearls and hobbled off
as fast as possible. The girls looked

at each other in amazement and continued on their way to the fair.

It was getting late as Snow White and Rose Red walked home, and the sun was just setting. To their surprise, they came across the dwarf again.

There, spread out on the ground in front of him was a great pile of gold and precious jewels. Suddenly, the dwarf saw the girls.

"Go away! You horrid girls are

always in my way," he shouted.
Suddenly there was a growl and
the bear stood by their side.
With one huge
paw the bear
swiped the
dwarf so far up
inlo the sky no
one ever saw
where he landed.
As the bear turned towards
Snow White and Rose Red, his

shaggy coat fell away. There stood a handsome young man. "Don't be afraid," he said. "That wicked dwarf put a spell on me so he could steal my treasure. You two have broken the spell with your kindness."

The girls were astonished and happy, and they all went home together with the treasure.

Snow White married the handsome young man who, by great good fortune, had a younger brother who married Rose Red. And they all lived happily ever after.

The End